My First Disney Story

This is a book for you to share with your child time and time again.

Read the story to your child, pointing to the words as you go. Encourage her* to look at the pictures, and talk about the story and what she can see. Ask questions about the action, and point out favourite characters. If your child is familiar with the story, she will enjoy telling you what is going to happen next! Encourage her to tell the story in her own words.

Above all, have fun sharing this favourite Disney tale with your child.

* To avoid the clumsy he/she and his/her we have referred to the child as she. All the books are, of course, equally suited to boys and girls, and all children will have their favourites.

A catalogue record for this book is available from the British Library

Published by Ladybird Books Ltd
27 Wrights Lane London W8 5TZ
A Penguin Company
LADYBIRD and the device of a Ladybird are trademarks of Ladybird Books Ltd
10 9 8 7 6 5 4 3 2 1
© Disney MM
Based on the Pooh stories by A A Milne (copyright The Pooh Properties Trust)

Disney's

THE Tigger MOVIE

Ladybird

It was autumn and Tigger bounced happily through the Hundred Acre Wood.

He bounced over to Pooh's house to see if Pooh wanted to go bouncing. But Pooh was too busy.

"I have to collect honey for the winter," Pooh said.

So Tigger bounced on, looking for someone to bounce with. But all his friends were too busy, getting ready for winter.

Poor Tigger! He felt all alone. But just then, Roo appeared.

"Tigger," Roo said, "maybe you're not alone. Maybe you have a family somewhere."

Tigger was very excited – a whole family of Tiggers! And so the two friends went to see Owl, to ask him how to find Tigger's family.

"To find your family, you must first find your family tree," Owl said.

But Tigger didn't understand what a family tree was. He thought it was a *real* tree! And so Tigger and Roo bounced off to the woods.

Tigger and Roo searched everywhere, but they couldn't find Tigger's family tree. At last, Tigger decided to go home.

As Roo bounced into Tigger's house, he crashed
into a cupboard. There he found a small locket.
Tigger held it up.

"This needs a Tigger family portrait inside," said Tigger. "Now, where could those other Tiggers be?"

"Why don't you write 'em a letter," suggested Roo, trying to cheer Tigger up.

And so that's what Tigger did. He dropped the letter into the postbox and waited... and waited... and waited.

Meanwhile, Tigger's friends were looking for Tigger's family, too. Pooh, Eeyore and Piglet found some bouncing creatures at the frog pond.

"They don't look like the right sort of Tiggers to me," sighed Pooh.

Then they found some stripey creatures, but they were bees!

Tigger was still waiting for a reply. Soon it began to snow and Roo had to go home.

"I wish I had a big brother like Tigger," Roo said to his mother that night.

"But he *is* one of our family," said Kanga. "As long as we care for him, he always will be."

Roo wanted to cheer Tigger up. So in the morning, he asked Pooh, Piglet, Eeyore, Kanga and Owl to write a letter. The friends pretended to be Tigger's family.

"Dress warmly," said Kanga.

"Eat well," added Pooh.

The friends knew that Tigger would like the letter.

The next day Tigger woke everyone up.

"Look what I've got!" he said happily. "A letter from my family. And they're all coming to visit me tomorrow."

Nobody remembered writing that in the letter! What were the friends to do?

Roo felt very guilty – Tigger was so looking forward to seeing his family. Then Roo had another idea.

"We'll dress up, act real tiggery and then Tigger will think we're his family!"

Everyone thought Roo's idea was perfect, and they began to get ready.

"Hoo-hoo-HOOO!" cried Tigger when the friends arrived at his house. "Let's bounce!"

Everyone bounced, but Roo tripped and his mask slipped. When Tigger saw it was Roo, he was very upset. He thought his friends were making fun of him.

"T-T-F-E – Ta-Ta-For-Ever," he said as he opened the door and disappeared into the night!

Roo was so worried about Tigger that he went to
see Pooh the next morning. Roo wanted to bring
Tigger home. So all the friends went out to
search for him.

Meanwhile, Tigger was in another part of the wood. Snow was falling all around him.

Tigger looked up and saw a magnificent tree.

"My family tree!" he cried. "Tigger family, are you there?"

But there was no reply. Tigger felt all alone. But he wasn't *really* alone. His friends were close by and Tigger was overjoyed to see them.

Just then, there was a rumbling noise and a huge pile of snow came sweeping towards the friends. Tigger quickly bounced everyone to safety. But he was swept away in the snow!

"I'll save you!" cried Roo. He bounced a huge bounce and rescued Tigger.

Tigger soon realised that his family had been there with him all along.

And when they got home, Tigger had a big party to say thank you to his friends. They were together again, as a family, in the Hundred Acre Wood.